Ta

th

Françoise Sabard

Ayo's Adventures
Tales of my journeys through
the Second Life virtual world

© 2009, Françoise Sabard
Edition : Books on Demand, 12/14, rond-point des Champs Elysées, 75008 Paris, France
Imprimé par : Books on Demand GmbH, Norderstedt, Allemagne

ISBN 978-2-8106-0772-3
Dépôt légal : avril 2009

I am Ayo. I am the Second Life© avatar of Fran in the Second Life virtual world[1]. For those of you how have never been to Second Life, SL is a melting pot where a thousand souls meet and part. It is the crossroads of many paths. It is a virtual world. People from Real Life indwell avatars through which they can exist in SL. Via SL, people leave their Real Life behind and take on a new existence in this electronic world. This gives them lots of benefits. For example, people who do not have legs can fly. Those who are alone can find company. Bored souls can add spice to the humdrum of their daily life. Shattered personalities feel they can put the pieces of the jig saw puzzles of their lives together again and of course, dreamers can dream. It sounds like paradise… But of course all paradises have their serpents.

I am not a human being, not flesh and blood, just an image. I should say… I am a shadow, or… let's say, the ghost of a real being. My alter ego is real and I am not. SHE puts words into my mouth and SHE voices opinions and expresses feelings, which happen to be HERS as well as MINE, and it annoys me at times as she tries to lead my life according to her criteria… no nonsense. Nevertheless, this is MY story. I want to tell you about MY experiences in Second Life.

---

1   Second Life is a Linden Research Inc. brand

As I said before I am the way that Fran can interact in this world. As an avatar, I don't have the limitations that Fran does. I can change my skin, hair and body shape as easily as Fran does her clothes, in fact easier. That is why people don't look like what they are; they look like what they choose to be. And people choose to be a lot of different things. Most people choose to appear as the kind of person that they wished they looked like in RL: who don't have all the flaws that they have in RL. In SL, to paraphrase Garrison Keilor, all men are strong and all women are supermodels. Some choose to change genders. Others to become animals, or have animal characteristics such as tails or animal ears. Others become mythological creatures, such as dragons or vampires. As an avatar, I don't have to eat, sleep or exercise. I can fly. As an avatar I don't age unless Fran decides that I should. I dare not mention the word immortality as everything about me is virtual and by definition I am non-existent.

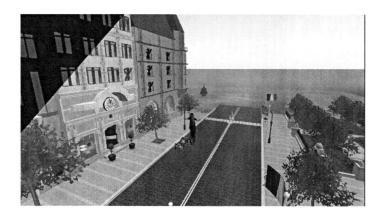

I was born a year ago. I was created because my original, who is a teacher, had read about second Life in a teenage magazine and she wanted to experience it to be able to have worthwhile discussions with her pupils. So she started imagining me and she found herself trying to give life to her alter ego. I have the same tastes and the same reactions... somehow we happen to be alike

When you happen to see me on Second Life, this is what I look like on your PC. I am rather tall with wild shoulder length red hair. My complexion is light and I have large misty blue-grey eyes; mermaid eyes, a little more original than Fran's real light brown eyes. My figure is slim but curvaceous, a little slimmer round the waist than Fran's. I have so many clothes in my wardrobe... I mean my inventory - that I often forget I have them and more pairs of shoes than Imelda Marcos. But I always end up wearing the same old favourites a pair of dark jeans and a leather shirt, volatile summer skirts or a selection of glamourous long dresses with of course sexy stiletto heels I wouldn't dream of dancing with in real life. This is also what Fran likes to wear most of the time.

Second Life is an archipelago. So many islands of different nature. A replica of the world, real and imaginary. You don't have to get into a car, train or plane and take hours to get somewhere. Simply put the address in to a teleport and "poof!" you are there. Thus I don't have any idea of what is near anything else. In fact, you cannot go from one place to another without the teleport. Thus it is like a series of islands in a archipelago with great gulfs fixed in between that you cannot cross.

I live in a wooden shack lost in a swamp somewhere in the middle of SL Territories. This is where I "rez". I mean where I come to life, second life of course, or should I say where I join all the other souls when Fran decides to switch on her computer and be on line. I normally sit on the porch. There is another rustic chair for whoever wants to come and talk, an empty bottle of beer and an old banjo close to the door. There is absolutely nothing inside the cabin, no furniture whatsoever because the bare necessities are not a must in Second Life. One of the window panes is broken and patched with old newspapers. But it is not important it is neither hot not cold in SL; just a little touch of pretended poverty and barrenness in a virtual world turns squalor into poetry. There in no physical suffering nor misery and dreamers can afford to roam around carefree. Far from the bondage of wealth and responsibility, far from the crushing weight and suffering of real misery.

I love listening to the toads croaking at sunset when the perfect disc glows and sinks into the ocean behind the shack. There is also the permanent squeaking of an old rusty weather vane, the rustling of leaves. It all has a taste of reality. I can even imagine the iodine scent of the sea breeze lingering over the sweet and sour emanations of the muddy surface of the lagoon still waters .

The places I go to in SL are places I am fond of but time consuming places in Real Life: dancing takes you a whole evening, listening to music can be a matter of several hours without mentioning the day after an evening out... lack of sleep... splitting headache after too much drink... A sheer waste of time. In SL, as I mentioned you can go for a minute or a day. Drink all you want with no hangovers. Second Life however takes a back seat to Real Life. When the phone rings, the doorbell, or an urgent errand comes up invariably Second Life session is put on hold.

So you will find me where the music and the atmosphere are good. Folk music mostly and dancing are my hobbies. SL is linked to the best radio stations and you can enjoy non-stop excellent music, be it from Ireland, the States, or Cuba… it is a sheer delight for a music lover. There is music to suit all tastes. (Well in Second Life, I can waltz beautifully for Fran… Which is both fulfilling and frustrating… as every time she has tried waltzing in real life, she has killed her partner's feet….)

You will find me mostly in Dublin pubs for example, or at the Junkyard in the South of the United States, strolling around in wooden gazebos enjoying crayfish and beer… I have also visited the world's capitals: Amsterdam, Paris, London. I also enjoy traditional places, wild west ranches or kingdoms of fantasy such as Avilion where fairies and other creatures of medieval legends can be found. SL places are similar to real ones but they lack this genuine bustling of life. If I recognize certain areas to which I have an emotional attachment because Fran knows them, however it is still artificial. Minute details are missing and to a certain extent, the context and the ambiance are different. Blarney in Dublin looks like an urban pub, but the people are not Irish, so it lacks the irishness of the pub. Monuments, public squares and gardens are somehow disincarnated. Towns and landscapes remain rough sketches as you can see in dreams. Buildings, roads, hills are stereotypes (How can it be otherwise?). Walking along SL streets of Dublin leaves the same bitter feeling of not being able to get hold of what I had originally come for… actually taking Fran back to the real Dublin she knows.

However, due to my lack of experience and due to the fact that I am rather outgoing, I landed in some unexpected and sometimes unwanted adventures. Let me tell you some of them.

Gender Bender Len

Once, I was sitting on the porch when I saw someone gliding past the shack on a bright red scooter.

"Do you want a ride?"

Len (his name) was my first encounter in Second Life.. We went to a Far East region and we walked together under the surface deep into the sea. We saw schools of fish, crabs crawling into antique amphoras and we stood there talking for ages, exchanging ideas and I felt attracted to him.. I really wanted to see him again… and I did see him again… He took me to a romantic island, to a grandiose ballroom with two grand pianos which does not exist any more. This is very much like life, the world goes round, time flies and things change. In the real world, people can't recognize places because they have run down dramatically over years. In Second life, it happens much faster and sometimes landscapes, buildings and all disappear in the blink of an eye, overnight.

I sat and started playing. Playing the piano has always been a dream of Fran's. Her daughter worked diligently to learn and now she plays beautifully. As Fran stubbornly refused to take lessons from an old aunt of hers, she can only have me play on a virtual keyboard any music she feels inside, and it comes out perfectly. However, she is frustrated and as I strongly think somehow, she is cheating.

Anyway, Len and I started dancing and he was whispering such nice things to me. I danced on and on, listening and enjoying it all as if it was real. The sweet tunes were pouring out of my Pc and I was happy in Len's arms, enjoying every second of it.

Obviously Len was older in SL and he knew all the tricks and he was quite a character. He was able to make the most of it. He was building boats... and other things... and giving other souls useful tips and landmarks about Second Life until one day I met him, or perhaps I should say her. Len was a woman and I got a shock, the first and biggest shock of my Second Life... I left him and I went to read his profile. This is an advantage of SL, you can read about someone through his profile... and indeed Len could be either a man or a woman in SL. I started reconsidering my view of him. He is still a very good friend but the little touches of romance he had initiated vanished for such is SL!... and I realized the danger of such interferences: Real feelings for a virtual being... real life attraction... to someone who remains a soul, a very human soul but to someone who remains hidden behind his avatar. It is just like getting attracted to Morpheus himself. Once a butterfly and the next day a slug. Are you supposed to adjust to his various aspects and moods? Maybe this is the solution... forgiveness and tolerance... in SL as well as in RL. It sounds like one of the first Christian principles, a very ancient recommendation indeed. Is it the Truth? The right path to peace?

True exchanges on SL are of intellectual nature. Sensual feelings and emotion can only lead to frustration or sheer disappointment on both sides. Fulfilment resides in intellectual exchanges, sheer friendship... just like correspondence in war times...? Worse than that... with the ultimate goal of remaining a dream... Souls are like illusions in the desert, nobody knows who is a male or a female avatar, who is honest who is playing a role. Can the avatar influence the behaviour of the person who remains behind, pulling the strings? The same person in a different form can behave differently as far as his true self can remain hidden. There is nothing solid to cling to... you just find your way in Second life all by yourself even more than in Real Life, you feel blindfolded. It sometimes feels like quicksand. You just have to trust the others and rely on your personal intuition... it is a risky venture..

Getting Thrown out of a House and a Life

The other encounter I have to talk about is an Australian soul called Keith. Things were so pleasant and smooth between us both and they remained so for a while. Keith was a newbie on SL and his avi was nothing sophisticated but his conversation was varied and interesting and I was really enjoying sitting around in paradises, and talking, talking around a cool drink!…

One day we came upon a beautiful house which I wanted to visit at all cost. It was the kind of house I would like to have in RL. A comfortable place with large French windows overlooking a wonderful garden, English style with a lot of shrubs and wild flowers and trees all around. The owner was called Claudius and I will always remember it. I figured he would let us just visit as long as he was not around as many landlords do in SL. So Keith and I went in, through the hall, to the sitting room. But once there, it was impossible to get out. The door wouldn't open, no way of going through the walls. I don't remember whether we thought of blinging off at that time. We were amazed and we felt like prisoners when suddenly someone flew in. He did not leave us. And worst of all, Keith had managed to get out and I was left alone with Claudius. He started shouting: "You are trespassing… How dare you… you slut…" And so on and so forth . He called me all kinds of names and treated me like a dog before opening the door to let me out. I ran out quickly and Fran put both hands on her ears not to hear anything else. How she hates violence! All sorts of violence… physical, verbal, silent violence… And suddenly, she was feeling so hurt and revolted, I turned back to face Claudius and I yelled on top of my voice: "Look you! I have not offended you in any way, I just wanted to have a look at your house, and now this is how you treat me...save all this for your enemies, or your slaves. I am neither and I feel sorry for you... I hope I will never see you again." I flew off, Fran shut her laptop. She was in a real rage, fuming... and she wondered at this point if Ayo and her were not the same person. All this had been directed against me and she was just not able to keep at a distance she was actually physically feeling my fury and she was involved in it.

The other similar experience was when I met Keith in a nice garden later on. We were having a cool drink and we were talking as we used to do. He started telling me about his real life his family and his dogs. He was living in Australia and he had a big house by the ocean. Then he said he wanted to stop seeing me on SL because he felt he was getting too much involved and we were going nowhere. I said it was OK and that we were only dreams on SL, but I understood then that behind each dream lay a real soul with a real ability to suffer. I have never seen Keith again... I suppose he must have decided to go back where he really belongs... With his family and growing children, his dogs. I can't blame him for this wise decision, but I cried... and I still feel a longing for this lost relationship with a beautiful Australian soul.

Knowing that virtual relationships can hurt, Fran was determined from then on not to let me get involved into any more nonsense. I went on exploring SL, just looking for acquaintances to talk to... and I did talk simply because Fran talks all the time in RL, about the weather, about the program for the weekend, films she wants to see and books she is reading. But she avoids the big issues and then I have to takeover. This is what happened when I met Keith and after he disappeared, I started roaming around SL, exploring new places but I was determined not to get too close to anyone. This heatbreak also helped me become aware that I was actually looking for my twin soul on Second Life, just like a teenager is waiting for the Prince Charming… in other words, I was dreaming within a dream… and that made me laugh at myself… Unbelievable Ayo!

So I went to music places I liked, and Fran was listening to her dear blues and going on with her work at home or at school while I was dancing away, answering questions when I heard them. Other souls must have been shocked at my lack of response.. but that is what I had become. The fact is I was still around in SL and I was still wandering…

Don't Talk to Gangstas My Girl!

And, one day, or one evening or whatever... it must have been full daylight for me, dawn for him and midnight in Second Life.. never mind. So I was saying that at the Blarney's, someone approached me and asked to dance with me. He was wearing what he called a "Chicago gangsta outfit". A striped suit and on his head a Borsalino hat which made him look ruthless.. and under this costume shone a bright soul. Sheer pleasure... His name was Ludwig. We have become very good friends mixing Second Life with Real Life. The truth oozed out... We started talking and among other things Ludwig decided to tell me about his perfect day and I was all ears. Let me tell you :

Ludwig's Perfect Day

Ludwig woke up in our bedroom standing beside our bed where he had been left the night before wearing the same clothes that he had worn then. He surveyed the perfect bed, which was perfectly made just as it always was, and their room was perfectly in order just as it always was. He sighed at the museum-like sterility of it all. He brightened when he saw the soft glow that meant I was waking up. As I "rezzed" into existence he said, "Good morning, beautiful!" He walked around the end of the bed and used animations from his inventory to kiss and hug me. When those animations ended, he clicked the bed and produced the love balls for us. I giggled and said, "nice thought! But we need to get some stuff done before we go to the party this evening" With that I pushed past him and went out of the room.

He sighed again. Sometimes it was tough to be a Second Life avatar. The Second Life world was freed of a lot of the social restrictions of the Real Life world but had its own limitations. In SL you can fly, moving from place to place is just a matter of entering the address and going immediately. You don't need to eat and can stay up indefinitely. On the other hand, you don't have the senses of touch, smell or taste and your movement capability is limited to running, walking and sitting.

He was the avatar of Mark, who is an American. While they met and could get together in SL, the time zone issues were enormous. He was on eastern US time and she was on Greenwich Mean Time, which meant that she was about 5-6 hours ahead of him depending on the time of year. When he got up it was lunchtime in France. When he finished work for the day, it was after midnight in France. They overcame this with a commitment to each other and him partially shifting his schedule so that he went to bed and got up earlier.

Ludwig would have given a lot to have the bed be messy or something out of place in the room to indicate that he had been there. What he would have given to have the morning's scenario play out this way:

He wakes up lying in the bed rather than just standing by it. He would be lying on a down mattress covered by a single sheet. The softness of the mattress would embrace him and caress him as he slept (avatars have no sense of feeling). Rolling over (he can't do that without an animation), he spies me laying there my back to him sleeping (this also requires an animation). He reaches out and traces the line of my spine with his fingers and then passes them over my behind to my thighs (this also requires a separate animation). Then he snuggles up to me and presses himself against me, his chest against my back and his manhood pressed into my rear. Hugging me to him, he kisses my neck and caresses my body and gently wakes me (another animation). I roll over onto my back and smile at him. He kisses me with increasing passion until I whisper in his ear to stop until the evening after the party.

He sighed again. While it is possible to create and link all these animations, it can't be done spontaneously. However, next he realized some of the advantages of SL. In the real world, he would have to get up, exercise and then take a shower before he could go out. However, in SL, his buff body never gets flabby so he doesn't have to exercise. It also doesn't need food so he doesn't have to eat and no matter what he does, he never gets dirty and has to take a shower. Most of all he's glad that he can do without the exercise, but he thinks it would be a great thing to join me in the kitchen making and eating breakfast together while discussing the news delivered to us over the internet.

As it is, all he has to do is change clothes to be ready to go shopping. This is done very simply in SL. He just drags an outfit that he has predefined for himself from his inventory to his body. SL removes the existing clothes and replaces them with the new clothes from the outfit. The concept of "clothes" includes such items as general body "shape" and the appearance of his body, his "skin", hair or lack there of. He doesn't have to use outfits, he could drag each piece of clothing separately but outfits make dressing easier.

After changing clothes, we go out shopping. Cancale being a small town we can walk out our door and down the street to the shops. Shopping is a much-simplified affair in SL. You walk in, point to what you want to buy and click to buy it. Stores look therefore like catalogs, pictures and lists of what is for sale. This all makes shopping very efficient but it also seems rather sterile to Ludwig . He would have liked to interact with a human or in this case avatar sales clerk, developing a relationship discussing what was going on in town, who was doing what, how his family was, but having a clerk would have just got in the way in terms of the transaction. Shopping is also simplified in what they shop for. Since we don't eat, we don't have to shop for food, so most of the shopping is for things like clothes, body accessories and home furnishing. Also since travel is so easy, we are not limited to the Cancale shops but can go to shops and malls all over SL simply by clicking a landmark. When we buy something, we receive items that are placed in our inventory lists. The inventory can contain small items like earrings but can also include items like ocean liners and castles! Because of digitalization, you can put a lot of big items into a very small space! He's happy about this since I seem to like to buy one of everything in the store especially shoes. He really doesn't provide a lot of input especially after the time he pointed out that I already had 300 pairs of black shoes and was informed that I needed these because they were Jimmy Choos! He mostly enjoys looking at me as I try on all the new outfits. Occasionally, he even buys something for himself.

After our shopping expedition, we return home. We could have stopped at a little café but not needing to eat or drink we didn't need refreshment and having spent the whole morning together, we didn't need to do any catching up. He missed that, it would have been nice to sit and watch the people, talk with the waiter while tasting the food. Sometimes at night we go to a pub to socialize with others and find out about their day. The Blarney Stone pub was our favorite but we also liked several other pubs. We liked to go in and sit on the bar stools and simultaneously drink symbols of various beverages and banter with our friends about many things.

Ludwig had a busy afternoon however. He had several conferences with his research collaborators on papers they were working on. These conferences were held by the several avatars meeting around a conference room in the office in their house. They would sit at the table and use the voice chat feature to discuss the paper. His conference table was setup to display various pieces of papers, drawings and multimedia that they would need to refer to. He could hear me playing the piano from downstairs. He smiled or would have if Ludwig had an animation for it because he knew that I loved playing. Fran loved it as well. Ludwig had bought the piano as a house-warming present for me when we finished the house. After the conferences were done, Mark closed the Second Life program and did some offline work.

He turned SL back on when it was time to go the party. There was no shared dinner. In SL, meals are generally de-emphasized since the avatars don't need to eat. Still Ludwig wished just like for breakfast that he could share the time with his wife. Also because travel is so quick in SL, people usually get ready for things just before event begins or even at the event. So we just pulled the outfits we wanted from inventory and teleported to the party. It was small affair of some writers who were to read parts of their latest work for comments from their friends, to listen to music and dancing. Music and dancing seem to be very popular in SL because music is the one medium that is the same in RL as it is in SL and thus is able to be directly similarly, dancing is a popular activity because there were a number of dances already programmed into SL so that dancers can select any number of dances and participate with proficiency. Combined with the fact that music is available concerts and dance parties are very popular.

At the party, Ludwig and I enjoyed a steamy IM session alternately making private caustic comments about the pieces we were hearing and flirtatious comments and statements what they were going to do to each other when they went home. During the dancing, we didn't dance with each other until the last dance, which did with slowdance 3. Holding and touching each other through a long slow song we continued to express our love and desire for each other, which was now growing quite strong. Quite rudely, we ignored other comments and IMs from others.

We walked back home pausing to kiss and touch along the way. When we got home, I surprised Ludwig by removing my clothes in front of him and running up the stairs to our bedroom. Ludwig recovering quickly removed his and followed me up. He found me already on the bed with love scene ball selected. He jumped on the blue ball and the animation took us through the steps of lovemaking until both Mark and Fran were satisfied. Ludwig however wished that he could be spontaneous like Mark and Fran. Unlike real life, he had to follow the script that was recorded in the love ball. He would have liked to be able make love to me as he wanted to but that wasn't possible.

After the love making, Mark selected the cuddle and sleep animation. Ludwig rolled over to his back and I nestled up next to him, my head on his shoulder, and my arm across his chest and one leg over his. Ludwig thought that this day was a perfect day and his life, as perfect as it gets. After further expressions of love, Mark and Fran closed 2nd Life and Ludwig and Ayo went into hibernation until they were started up again.

As days go by, Mark and Fran will be meeting and discussing on the net through Ludwig and myself. We will be together, going out, having fun, just like that the other day when we went to The Seychelles (French Zone). We danced and fought and wrestled in the mud to a point I found myself under Ludwig at his mercy in a game that was getting close to love-making, very intimate indeed! Mark and Fran were attending a predefined performance. They were not in control and they stood there watching… reacting maybe the same way, shivering on their own side of the Atlantic, miles away from each other.

Ludwig is my idea of a man, rough and tough with a dream face and a rocklike reassuring mental balance. He has Johnny Depp's triangular face and very blue eyes and I must be his ideal of a woman judging from his perfect day. However, Mark and Fran are far from this utter dream. They both have years of their own lives behind them with happy moments, hardships and disappointment. They have their families close to them. Chances are they could treasure their Second Life relationship as something that could have happened or is actually taking place in another dimension. What seems important now is to keep the present fire of their souls' encounter burning and this requires a lot of mental stability, serenity and determination. Building a meaningful relationship on Second Life is just like walking on a rope with hesitant steps forward with the risk of being suddenly thrown off balance by the slightest gust of wind, for such is the Second Life ballet of feeling

Robots and Space Guns in the Changing Room

Another issue on Second life is money.

I soon started to know where to find freebies with the help of more experienced souls. I beachcombed all the places to find what I needed. It was great fun even if I spotted glamourous expensive items I decided to make do with the free ones. It is amazing how designers can make good money in Second Life. Souls are as attracted to shopping as in Real Life, it is even worse. A lot of old SL citizens don't bother to use changing booths and try their new clothes shamelessly on the public place. SL is the end of all inhibitions. But I went to a discreet place to try my new outfits and shoes. For some reason roaming around naked has never been my cup of tea and I remain shy… it is a matter of self-respect. Even in SL Fran does not allow me to change anywhere as she still laughs when she remembers this episode of her life in Africa. Once her car stalled in front of the entrance of a nudist camp in Ivory Coast. The Ghanaian houseboy and driver got out, he opened the bonnet to look at the engine and suddenly, he bent and almost disappeared. Fran noticed a nudist standing behind the gate. After tightening the belt, the driver came back to the car, looking very angry and he said making wild gestures with the spanner he was holding: "Look Madam, white men have spent ages teaching us black people that we have to be dressed to be civilized… and now they go walk around naked… no be fit to be white men! No be good oh!"

So I found The Junkyard: a desolate area full of toxic waste. With tyres burning producing thick clouds of smoke. I settled under a massive concrete bridge, between two derelict shacks, which looked deserted.

I dragged my boxes from my inventory to the floor where they were not refused. I started opening them one by one. I put on a pair of jeans and a T-shirt. I chose high shoes, white ones with snake skin ankle bands and I carefully replaced the other clothes and accessories into my inventory. When I turned round to take a few steps, I felt closely spied on and I noticed a tiny robot, purring next to me. I greeted him and walked away. The little soul purred on. Then I spotted an aggressive looking being getting closer. He was wearing a mock soldier's uniform, a kind of battledress. He was holding a weapon from outer space something more sophisticated than a machine gun and his eyes were glittering deep inside the wide sockets of a skull like face. He focused his burning gaze on me . At that point, Fran really went all cold inside and she blinged poor me away from the creature. There are virtual places where you do not fit. They give you the creeps… just like Real Life when you go home late and you have to cross unsafe areas, almost running and clinging to the lapels of your coat for protection!

The Devil Lives in Aspen

This episode reminded me of a trip to SL Aspen. I had landed on a place surrounded by benches and fir trees. It was snowing , it was dark. There was nobody around and the place was dimly lit by four street lights.

I was trying to find a way to a civilized place with life, people, shops, when suddenly I saw him, crouching on one of the benches. He was sitting on one of his hind legs and holding his other knee with two tiny paws. He looked like a tiny malicious monkey with red eyes and pointed ears and two little horns. His tail was swaying to and fro like an angry cat. He was just like a taught little ball of fire, just ready to pounce. This soul was the Devil, bearing no name on top of his head nor group tag… It was then real cold sweat and Fran blinged me off back to her laptop and she sighed with relief in the warmth of her sitting room, back to secure reality.

Beware of the underworld very present on Second Life. it sends shivers down my spine. Evil is rampant in some dark islands, with all its cunning ways of attracting disciples. Vampire communities claim to be gentle and friendly while their members hunt for blood all over SL. Virtual blood and souls but the whole idea is unhealthy in itself.

All religions and churches are also represented. The choice is such a wide maze for young or weak minds!

Check Your Claws at the Door

I have not told you yet about my interest in fantastic creatures and imaginary world. Fran has devoured The Lord of the Rings, Harry Potter because of the children and she is a great fan of Walt Disney. There are special places in Second life where you can find yourselves way back in the Middle Ages for example in Avilion, there is a role play area and souls have to wear appropriate Middle Age costumes to be admitted. I once went into a forest where I found all kinds of interesting friends, knights, princesses, fairies… peaceful people talking and listening to music. Then I went to Avilion Grove grand ballroom. I was going in when the hostess Lady Do greeted me as usual and prevented a vampire from following me . This soul, frightening as he was, livid, with deadly fangs and long skeletal hands made even longer by lethal claws, started crying blood tears and protesting that he meant no harm. He just wanted to dance… and look around.

Lady Do accepted to let him in on the condition he would remove his claws. He pathetically refused saying that he would look ridiculous without them.

The hostess showed him the way out and he went and sat miserably on one of the stairs, all wrapped up in his cloak, with the sad and vacant gaze of people who have lost everything. Because of his attitude, the way he shrank in a corner like a sprayed spider, ready to die, I felt sorry for the creature… the Beauty and the Beast… and I started talking to Lady Do and pleading for him.

She raised her face to look at me, because she was very small, fluttering around with beelike wings and she firmly said "No way! He is a vampire! He is evil!"

I did not insist and I went in.

I feel so much for unhappy and scarred people, I always have to try and help and Fran gathers all kinds of morally dependent people around her.. and only God knows, she has a lot to work on for herself!

Violating the Rules

And I wondered how come SL was able to create such vivid feelings and reactions. I thought of the power of good books, films, and I thought that SL offered one more feature: interaction. Vanishing is my reaction most of the time but fighting back can be another and, people can express themselves in SL despite any rules.

Despite any rules! This is why I decided to build myself a little house on SL.

I used to go dancing in an old blues place called the House of Tunes where the music was so good Fran would let it play for ages while ironing or being busy in her RL house.

This hall was built in a hangar on a hill. There was a village with a bikers' bar by an old jetty on the sea front and I could get to the House of Tunes on a winding road up the hill.

Getting to the top, there were woods overlooking the ocean. I got to a small clearing in the middle of an old oak forest and I decided to set my home there.

I arranged my little bungalow facing the ocean and furnished it with love. There was even a rocking chair on the porch, but on that day I sat on the sofa in the living room and enjoyed a great peace… listening to the blues streaming out of the House of Tunes.

It was the only opportunity I had to enjoy my little home. The next time I went on SL, I was advised in a stern IM (instant message) that my house had been discarded and that I had been for ever banned from the House of Tunes. I tried to apologize to the author of the message to no avail. She was merciless and I was indeed doomed as far as the House of Tunes was concerned. In fact I have a feeling the House of Tunes does not exist any more. It was taken over by a group of bikers, maybe re-named… The Crossroads.. and they have forgotten all about me as I could enter the parcel with Ludwig the other day.

Beautiful people and money

However, homeless me, poor as a church mouse, I have met people with beautiful properties on SL. They must have invested quite a lot of their own money and real time to achieve their dreams. I would like to have a big house of my own with some land, horses… a flashy fast car… but if it means spending quite a lot to own virtual properties… which can disappear or be altered any time any day, is the risk worth it? And how long can one really enjoy a home in SL? No longer than a few hours a day…

Jerry and his wife own a ranch and other houses. Anna has a nightclub and she is an Interior decorator, she also sells houses, the original villa has been cloned and stretched or shrank to fit all possible sizes and therefore prices under different tags: Italian for sure, modern maybe, but certainly not French. Her husband Kerry is a photographer and I believe he also has a business running via Second Life.

No doubt these businesses in SL are linked to some extent to real life activities. I can imagine it is also possible to really advertise through SL via websites. Fran once heard on her French local radio station about a new island called Euskal Herria. She sent me on a recky but apart from a few typical buildings, there was nothing outstanding yet. I don't know whether I could one day become interested. I guess Fran is just a poor writer and translator and I fear I will remain the same Ayo and keep drifting along.

SL is also a place of knowledge. There is a whole library and some parts have connections with famous American universities. Students can work on Second Life... conferences are held. It should also be possible to publish books on line. I will enquire and let Fran know about it.

Writing is a pleasure for Fran as well as an outlet for inbuilt steam. In fact she will only stop writing when she is dead. She does not need to write for a living but writing is essential to her life just like oxygen.

Her relationship to money is quite strange. She likes money when she has it to make life more pleasurable for herself and people around her but she does not crave for money...maybe because the little she has is enough all the more as she no longer has to cater for her children. I, Ayo have never had children and never will and I am quite happy to live free on Second Life. If I really feel like buying something I will look for the money trees or get ready to sit for a while on a money chair. It is all part of the game.

Some girls will work as escorts or hostesses. I am not ready for this at all. Besides, Fran does not have enough time for a full time job on Second Life.

I have even noticed that avatars have the possibility to become pregnant in SL and go through the different stages of pregnancy. This goes to show that SL is a means of getting one's dreams close to reality and making one's wishes come close to true... but... to end up dealing with utmost frustration of something left unfinished for good

Once, I also made a personal effort to honour an invitation to a wedding. An Irish friend of mine was getting married on SL. It was quite a ceremony. It looked like a wedding in Las Vegas. The bride was glamorous in her white candy floss dress and it lasted quite a while before we proceeded to the reception hall. I was with an English lady, very British indeed under a gracious hat, and we had a friendly chat which was quite close to reality, mainly the new couple and the weather! One question arises though: where are the limits? Is all this a question of mere role-play? Do souls get trapped in these illusions?

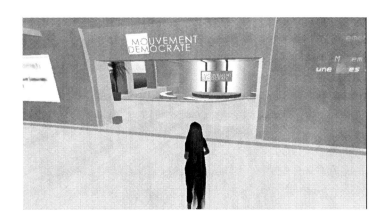

Ayo and Politics

Let me tell you now about my experience of political circles too. Most public figures have their sites and their groups in Second Life and I have been made Deputy for France on SL by a friend who actually paid for my membership as you know I am the brokest tramp in SL. I am ashamed to say that I have never got myself round to attend any meeting whatsoever whether or not I was interested in the issue for selfish reasons… Fran resents useless meetings when people blow hot hair and nothing concrete comes out. She must have passed it on to me.

At the time of the French presidential election I became a member of the adverse parties clubs for sheer curiosity's sake and most of the time I was disappointed by the poor quality of most debates on both sides… only a few were satisfactory. Now in the heat of the US presidential election I have noticed that both parties are very present in Second Life but I will keep my political opinions to myself since they are Fran's anyway.

Interaction of Second Life and Real Life feelings… I exist in another dimension and I tend to invade Fran's life and soul at unexpected moments when I feel like waking up from my forced hibernation because I have, or Fran has something important to share with Ludwig/Mark: a new story, a piece of music or anything else imported from Real Life for that matter. I am not a bionic creation, there is no possibility of my developing a mind of my own just like Frankenstein but I have the power of dimming the limits between Real Life and Second Life. Besides, Ludwig and I have created a current and a real flow of intellectual exchange between us. Just writing about my adventures, sharing ideas, feelings to a point of getting to know each other more and more each day.

Fran may feel like killing me, just like Conan Doyle got tired of Sherlock Holmes and decided to have him die after so many episodes, for the simple reason that I am taking too much of her time and life… however, she will still be haunted by memories of the wonderful time we had with Ludwig/Mark on SL.

Nothing is in control

One day I met Ludwig at the Junkyard. It was after. I had an IM (important message). He had come home at the shack, missed me and he wanted to see me. As usual I was eagerly expecting him, wondering what he would have to tell me. I had lots to talk about and I was looking forward to seeing him again.

When he appeared, he suggested we went to the Junkyard. I happily agreed and off we went. He chose a salsa. We always did wonders at the Junkyard. The music carried us and no other couple could perform better (Just an illusion!) – Suddenly,I noticed a change in Ludwig's tone. He sounded dead serious all of a sudden. He urged me to listen to him. I was all ears. I was not expecting anything in particular but I felt a strange shiver run down my spine while reading his words.

Then, he told me, ever so delicately. I could tell he was afraid to hurt me. In fact he was trying to kill me with a feather. He explained that we could not go beyond friendship because of our mutual ties to loved ones in Real Life. We were just an extension of Mark and Fran and in that respect any bound other than work and friendship would be a mistake.

I stood there and admired how accurate his analysis was compared to what I was just confusedly feeling. I had drifted as usual and Fran had not done anything to prevent me from responding to Ludwig' s affection.

I thought the time had come to take a stand and Ludwig was taking the right steps… as I was saying earlier on… there is no future in Second Life… we are dreams… just dreams.. and I suddenly woke up to the fact that Ludwig was preserving the sanity of our relationship and preventing it from becoming nothing more than a glittering mirage in the desert. Sound friendship was indeed the right way.. the right way is rougher but it is always the best and Ludwig was one of these rare souls, capable of chosing "la porte étroite" as André Gide wrote: the narrow path.

The Underworld

So we parted and I went home to the shack..I sat there indulging in a state of utter despair. The little friendly cabin had suddenly turned into a desert island.

I sat on the porch. This time it was no use expecting Ludwig to rez by my side. I was on my own all frozen inside.

A few avatars landed and tried to talk to me. I remained polite and distant as I was mentally so far away..

Then a tall girl dressed in red and black drew my attention and came next to me. She asked for my help and I answered I would do my best provided her request was within my reach.

-"I am in need of blood, she said, will you let me bite you?

- Are you a vampire? I asked

- Yes I am.

- Come closer, I added, let me see your face. You don't look frightening to me!

- I am actually wearing fangs but you can't see them unless I bite… and am getting very thirsty indeed, I feel very faint.

- Ah! I said, I would love to help but I cannot donate my blood because I was in England during the Mad Cow Disease epidemic. So, if you are ready to run the risk… lol ☺"

I was joking, the conversation was very light-spirited but I was thinking that I had lost my dear Ludwig and I could not care less for anything else. In fact becoming the shadow of a living dead on Second Life and losing my soul there would dramatically put an end to anything sensible.

It was late in the night and "the big fat moon was shining like a spoon" above the shack as Bob Dylan sang. The other chair on the porch was desperately empty and the old banjo was silently resting against the wall close to the old empty bottle of booze. I thought about Ludwig's tall figure suddenly showing up and I wish I had tears to cry out my pain. I told the vampire :

- "Alright Martine, go ahead! One question though. Shall I become a vampire once I have been bitten?

- No, she answered, I cannot do that, you will have to decide whether you want to join us eventually...

- I will think about it." were my last words before she pounced on me. As she opened her mouth wide I saw her eyes shrink and redden like those of a hungry wolf and she planted her fangs into my neck. I was crying as I was feeling my life and my pain flow out of my body into the vampire's.

I remained alone on the porch with my head down. "Away" cried the little tag above my head, and Fran put me to sleep.

Second Life goes on

As time went by, I kept exploring Second Life islands. The Blarney still played its traditional Irish music, and the Junkyard radio wailed the Blues but everything seemed drab without the excitement of Ludwig's company and his lively conversation. I was missing his comments and his presence so much, until one day he started showing up at the shack. It was almost like when we first met, then he joined me in our different places. He once found me dancing with another avi and told me he was almost jealous. Is this kind of jealousy a feeling that should arise between mere friends? We went on with our meetings and conversations. I wonder whether Ludwig realized that we were in fact resuming our previous relationship while denying the fact that we wanted to be nothing more than friends.

He was telling me about getting a place in Second Life. He had actually started chatting me up again despite his own will. Fran and Mark were of course keeping quiet behind their laptops. None of them put his foot down because of the way both of us had started carrying on a dangerous path once more. Can you tell me why? Simply because Second Life is very tricky and it can easily take you where you have no intention to go under the pretense that avatars are only dreams.

Fran and Mark, please never underestimate Ayo and Ludwig! SL is no child play and this is why youngsters and weak adults should think twice before indulging in impossible relationships or perversions of all kinds.

One needs to be very clear analyzing avatars' actions and reactions and it can be quite a fight between personal pulsions and what has to be.

Ludwig is going to hibernate a little to let Mark enjoy

Thanksgiving. And in the meantime I am trying to sort out things on paper with Fran.

And again in the meantime, I had interesting discussions with a leopard and an owl. Fancy that! I used to dream about it when I was a child! Talking to the animals is possible on Second Life. This leopard was a poet and I loved what he wrote. The owl had a lot of trouble having its language translated into English. What do you expect? The automatic translator did an awful job and it had to quit out of desperation.

The Boat

This morning I woke up telling myself I was tired of being a mere tramp on Second Life. Ludwig had taken the trouble of showing me beautiful properties, furnished and unfurnished. I had seen a few myself. In fact we had visited one shortly before Fran had to leave in a hurry and let me hibernate for five good days. I was supposed to enquire about the rent and other amenities but Fran was in such a state when she came back that she did not have the heart to send me on any further errand.

So I went wandering about online as usual. Ludwig had mentioned a few prices which did not seem outrageous, although I still had this fear at the back of my mind which had always prevented me from engaging in any financial venture on Second Life. I ended up at The Junkyard Blues club. My twin soul was nowhere to be seen. A few avis were dancing salsa, slow numbers to the same tune which did not fit any of their movements. Fran was laughing at the scene but I suddenly got nervous and listless and I started walking away to the beach. I saw rows of mobile homes. Some of them were for rent and quite cheap but I did not take the trouble to step inside as I remembered Ludwig had never shown any enthusiasm at this idea.

Then I walked on towards the Marina, past a score of houseboats squatting in a line just like a family of ducks. I strolled to the last one. The view over the ocean was so wonderful.There was a tiny island planted with coconut trees darkening in the glowing twilight. The rent was 800 Linden $ per week! Quite affordable provided the said week referred to a real time span. I made sure of it and Fran proceeded to the visa transaction: real money into Linden $. Sheer heresy..! Against all my previous principles! Then I went on board to make sure the inside was as I thought it was. Basic and very cosy. The sitting room was spacious with large windows equipped with venetian blinds. There was a comfortable sofa in front of a warm fireplace, a bit unusual on a boat... but for the sake of creating a cosy ambiance. The kitchen was functional.

The beauty of this boat was the upper floor. I climbed up the ladder, I saw the large bedroom with a door to the deck and I lay down outside under the sunshade. Full view over the ocean beyond the tiny island... Too good for words! I had turned on the radio downstairs and my soul was rocked, just like The Boat, by the bluest of New Orleans blues. What a peaceful place to come and rest away from the wicked world, real and unreal. I jumped up, run down the ladder and clicked on the sign board to rent The Boat. I dreaded Ludwig's reaction but I had made up my mind. I had fallen in love with The Boat.

When I saw him his reaction was not too much of a shock, he knew me and although he had something more suitable in mind for Mark and their activities on Second Life, he sounded very happy about spending time with me on The Boat, talking, listening to music with crayfish and beer.. and I will not talk about what else he had in mind!

As I was no longer a tramp, I teleported to the shops and I was determined to find glamourous hair. I went to hundreds of places and nothing was right as I has a predefined idea of the type of hair I wanted. I finally came across a Mermaid Shop and I immediately set my choice on long sleek auburn hair and I felt right wearing it.

Then I longed to see Ludwig... I wanted him to approve of The Boat, of my new face. I hadn't seen him for a while. I guess Mark must be busy at this time of year.

I went back to The Boat and as I rezzed upstairs I noticed Ludwig's tall figure on the deck. I love it when I find him waiting for me at the shack and now on board The Boat. As he admired my new hair, I was praying to live hundreds more of these moments of reunion... later on we went dancing at the Junkyard Blues South, next to the Marina. He asked me if I had ever thought of stripping in Second Life. I said I couldn't possibly and he made me promise never to do it . This was not difficult for me as I am of a reserved and shy nature and I was in raptures to think he cared, and on we were dancing in harmony when suddenly First Life rudely interrupted us...

Should there be a conclusion?

Fran and Mark remain miles away from each other and we take off to meet on the web in another dimension. But the impact created by these meetings echo like the rings made by a stone on the surface of the water and touch our real souls, those of Fran and Mark, whether they like it or not.

They will have to decide whether they can put up with their alter egos in another dimension. As grown ups, they will sort it out…

I will either live or burst like a bubble in the sun… deep in my heart, I want to live on and I am not ready to give up seeing Ludwig.

Fran will have the last word as far as I am concerned and Mark will deal with Ludwig…

We still don't know what these last words will be… for such is the power and the spice of Second Life… a serious adult game…

I have not explored all there is to know in Second Life and chances are I will never be able to check everything. It is so vast! I am sure Ludwig has visited more of this virtual world than I will ever do…

As long as we are online, it is a never ending story… and I seem to remember I have a date with Ludwig tomorrow…

Printed in the United States
145923LV00003B/6/P